The Wolf and his Shadow

and other Aesop's Fables

Compiled by Vic Parker

Miles Kelly

First published in 2013 by Miles Kelly Publishing Ltd
Harding's Barn, Bardfield End Green, Thaxted, Essex, CM6 3PX, UK

Copyright © Miles Kelly Publishing Ltd 2013

2 4 6 8 10 9 7 5 3 1

Publishing Director Belinda Gallagher
Creative Director Jo Cowan
Editorial Director Rosie McGuire
Designer Joe Jones
Production Manager Elizabeth Collins
Reprographics Stephan Davis, Jennifer Hunt, Thom Allaway

ISBN 978-1-84810-941-4

Printed in China

British Library Cataloguing-in-Publication Data
A catalogue record for this book is available from the British Library

ACKNOWLEDGMENTS
The publishers would like to thank the following artists who have contributed to this book:
Cover: Marco Furlotti
Advocate Art: Natalie Hinrichsen, Tamsin Hinrichsen
The Bright Agency: Marcin Piwowarski
Frank Endersby
Marco Furlotti
Jan Lewis (decorative frames)

Made with paper from a sustainable forest

www.mileskelly.net   info@mileskelly.net

www.factsforprojects.com

Contents

The Swan
and the
Goose

There was once a rich man who wanted to show off to his neighbors. He went to market and bought a goose and a swan. He fed the goose well, making sure it grew plump, ready to be cooked for a feast one day. However, he planned to keep the swan, so he could hear its beautiful song from his window.

The time finally arrived for the man to hold his feast. His cook and kitchen assistants worked hard in preparation to make many delicious dishes. Then they had to kill the goose ready for cooking. So that night, the cook went out to catch it. He could hardly see his hand in front of his face, let alone tell one bird from the other. By mistake he caught the swan instead of the goose. The swan, knowing it was about to be killed, burst into one last beautiful song. The cook realized that he had the wrong bird — and so the swan was saved by its singing.

Sweet words may save us from danger, when harsh words fail.

The **Frogs** who **Wanted** a **King**

Once upon a time, there was a group of frogs who lived as happily as could be in a marshy swamp. Not many animals would enjoy the boggy conditions, but it suited the frogs.

Every day, they went splashing about through the puddles, without a care in the world. No one came near the slimy, grimy waters, so no one troubled them. But some of the frogs thought that this happy-go-lucky life was not right, that they should have a king and proper rules. So the frogs prayed to the great god

Zeus, who ruled over the Earth, to give them what they wanted.

"Mighty Zeus," they cried, "please send us a king who will rule and keep us in order."

High up on Mount Olympus, where the gods and goddesses lived, Zeus laughed at the noisy croaking of the frogs.

'A king?' he thought. 'What would those silly creatures do with a king?' Instead, he threw down into the swamp a huge log, which landed with a SPLASH in the water.

The frogs were frightened out of their lives! They all rushed to the bank to see whatever had fallen from the sky. At first they thought it must be a horrible monster. But after a time, seeing that it did not move, one or two of the boldest frogs ventured out toward the log, and even dared to touch it. Still it did not move.

Then the bravest of the frogs jumped upon the log and began dancing up and down on it. All the other frogs soon came and did the same. After that, they lost interest in the log. For some time they went about their business without taking any notice of the log lying in their midst.

But they still wanted a king. So they prayed to Zeus again, and said to him, "Please send us a king – not just a log, but a real king who will really rule over us."

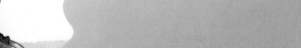

This irritated Zeus. 'How ungrateful and foolish they are,' he thought. So he sent a big stork that set to work gobbling up all the frogs. Then they wished they had never asked for a king in the first place, but it was too late.

Better no rule than cruel rule.

The Two Men and the Bear

Once upon a time, two men were traveling through a wood together, chatting about this and that to pass the time. All at once, a huge, bear rushed out at them.

The travelers were of course terrified. One ran for his life. He dashed into a thicket of trees, seized hold of the low-hanging

branches and gathered them around him to hide himself. The other traveler threw himself to the ground, face-down in the dust. He kept still, not even daring to breathe. The bear came up to him, sniffing him all over. But at last with a growl it slouched off. It thought the man must be dead, and bears do not like dead meat.

Then, when the man in the trees saw that the bear had gone, he came out and returned to his companion. Laughing, he said, "What was it that the bear whispered to you?"

"It told me," said the other, "a friend who runs off and leaves you at the first sign of trouble should not be trusted."

Never trust a friend who deserts you at a pinch.

The Workman and the Nightingale

It was a hot summer's night – so hot that a workman could not get to sleep. Instead, he lay with the window open, hoping that a little breeze might blow through, listening to the beautiful song of a nightingale. The little bird kept him company all night long, singing sweetly. The workman listened intently, and he was so delighted by its singing that he decided he had to have the bird for himself.

The next night, the workman set a trap for the nightingale and captured it. "Now that I

have caught you," he cried, "you will always sing to me, whenever I want."

But the little bird held its chin high and proud and shook its head. "We nightingales never sing in a cage," it said.

"Then I will eat you," said the workman. "I have always heard that a nightingale on toast is a tasty snack."

The nightingale quivered in terror. "No, please don't eat me!" it begged. "Let me go free, and I will tell you three things that are worth far more than my little body."

The workman thought for a moment, but he didn't see how he could lose. "All right," he shrugged, and he set the bird free.

Without a moment's hesitation the nightingale flew up to the highest branch of a nearby tree and looked down at the workman,

way out of reach below.

"The three things are pieces of advice," it trilled. "Firstly, never believe a captive's promise. Secondly, keep what you have. And thirdly, don't feel sad for what you have lost forever and cannot get back."

Then, while the workman was wondering how he could have been tricked by a tiny bird, the nightingale flew away.

Do not feel sorry about what is lost forever.

The Hare
with many
Friends

There was once a hare who was popular with the other animals. She was good-natured and fun to be with. Everyone claimed to be her friend. But one day she heard the sound of thundering hooves and howling hounds – huntsmen were approaching with sniffer dogs. The hare knew they were after her. What if she could not outrun them? She thought her friends might be able to help her escape instead.

So the hare ran off to see the horse, and asked him to carry her away from the hounds on

his back. But he refused, stating that he had work to do for his master. "I'm sure," he said, "that the bull would be happy to help you."

So the hare dashed off to ask the bull, hoping that he would charge at the hounds with his horns. But the bull replied, "I am very sorry, but I have an appointment. However I feel sure that the goat will do as you ask."

The hare sped off to see the goat. However, he feared that his back might be too bumpy for the hare. "I don't want to

hurt you," he explained. "Why don't you ask the ram? His back is wooly and soft."

So the hare hurried to see the ram and told him about the hunters. The ram replied, "My friend, I do not like to interfere, as hounds have been known to eat sheep as well as hares."

The hare was growing desperate. The sound of the hunt was getting ever closer. She sprinted off to see the calf, as a very last hope. However, the calf said that he too was unable to help. He did not like to take the responsibility, as so many adults had declined the task.

By this time the hounds were very near. There was nothing left for the hare to do but run for her life – and luckily, she escaped.

She that has many friends, has no friends.

The Wolf and his Shadow

There **was once a big, hairy wolf,** who was roaming across a plain at the end of a day's hunting. The sun was low in the sky, and the wolf noticed that his shadow was enormous.

"I knew I was big, but I didn't realize I was that big!" said the wolf to himself. "Why, I am a very fine creature indeed. Everyone should be afraid of me – and I should be afraid of no one. Fancy me bowing down to a lion! I ought to be King of the Beasts." Not caring about any danger, the

wolf began strutting along as if he was the finest animal on Earth. But just then a lion pounced upon him, seized him in his jaws, and began to eat him. "Alas," the wolf cried, "had I not lost sight of the facts, I shouldn't have been ruined by my fancies."

Be realistic about your own potential.

19

The **Bat**
and the
Weasels

A **bat once lived** with his fellow bats in a
deep, dark cave. They lived happily, flying
out to hunt at night and returning to sleep
during the day. However one evening, the bat
flew into a tree and fell to the ground.
Unfortunately, a weasel sniffed him
out. Before the bat could fly

away, the weasel had pounced and caught him.

The bat begged to be let go. The weasel said he couldn't do that because he was an enemy of birds. "I'm not a bird, I'm a mouse," said the bat.

The weasel looked at the bat. "So you are," he said, "now I look at you," and he let the bat go.

Soon after, the bat was caught in the same way by another weasel, and begged for his life.

"No," said the weasel, "I never let a mouse go."

"I'm not a mouse," said the bat, "I'm a bird."

The weasel examined the bat. "So you are," he said, and he too let the bat go.

Look and see which way the wind blows before you commit yourself.

The **Trumpeter** taken **Prisoner**

Once, during a time of war, there was a brave army trumpeter who went too close to the enemy on the battlefield. Enemy soldiers captured him and dragged him back behind their lines, delighted that he could no longer sound out the other side's orders. The soldiers were about to put him to death, when the young trumpeter begged for mercy.

"Look at me – I am not a fighter," he said. "I don't even carry a weapon. All I do is blow this trumpet – and how can that hurt you? So I ask you, why do you want to kill me? Please spare my life, I have done nothing to you."

But the enemy soldiers answered grimly, "You may not have had a hand in the fighting against us, but by sounding out the orders, you guide and encourage your soldiers in battle. They and you have killed hundreds of our men, so now you must pay the price for your music."

Those who stir up trouble are as guilty as those who carry it out.

The Tuna-fish and the Dolphin

Once upon a time in the ocean, far out in deep water, a dolphin was chasing a tuna-fish. They both splashed through the water at a great rate, swimming with all their might, and gradually the dolphin began gaining on the tuna-fish.

Just as the dolphin was about to seize him, the tuna-fish gave a huge leap that carried him right out of the water and onto a sandbank. In the heat of the chase the dolphin followed him, and there they both lay out of the water,

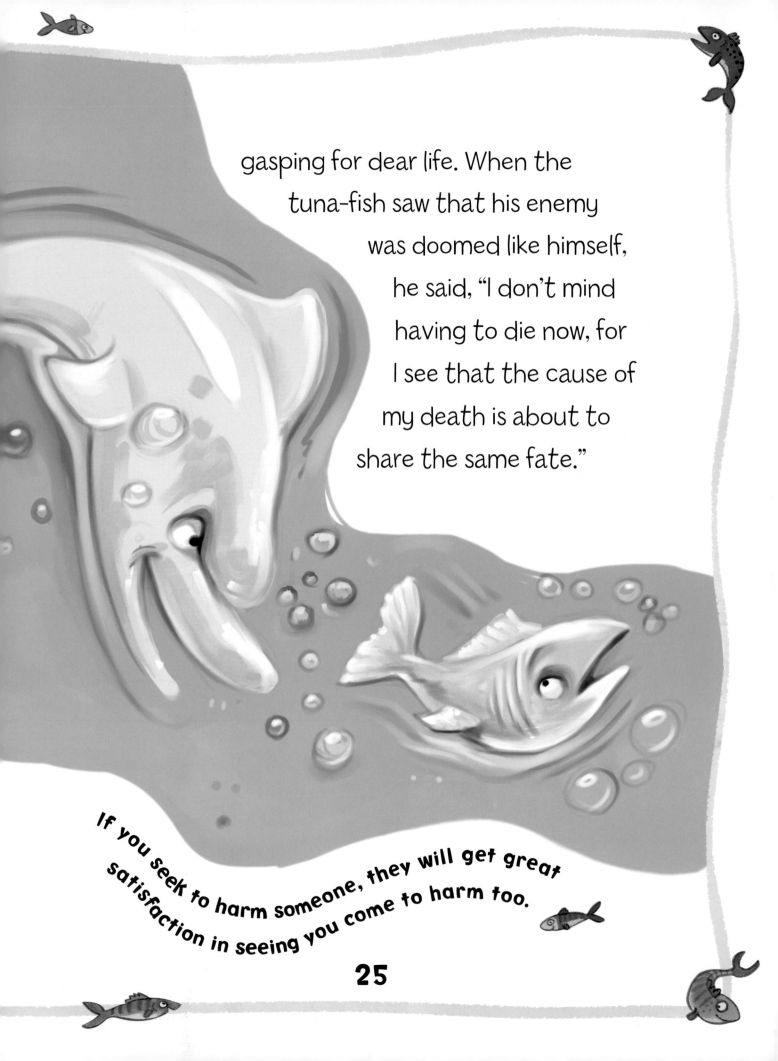

gasping for dear life. When the
tuna-fish saw that his enemy
was doomed like himself,
he said, "I don't mind
having to die now, for
I see that the cause of
my death is about to
share the same fate."

If you seek to harm someone, they will get great
satisfaction in seeing you come to harm too.

The
Bee-Keeper

There was once a bee-keeper who had many hives full of honey. A thief had his eye on them and was determined to steal the honey for himself. He waited until the bee-keeper went out one day, then broke in and stole every last morsel from the hives.

When the bee-keeper returned and found the hives empty, he was very upset. It wasn't long before the bees came back from gathering nectar and, finding their hives overturned and the keeper standing by, they thought it was he who had taken all their honey. In their rage, they stung the bee-keeper, swarming over him. At this the bee-keeper was furious and cried, "You ungrateful scoundrels, you let the thief who stole my honey get away with it and then you sting me, the person who has always taken such care of you!"

If you hit back, make sure you have the right person.

The Apes and the Two Travelers

Once upon a time, two men were traveling on a journey together. One of the men always spoke the truth, but the other never said anything but lies.

After some time, they came to a land of apes. The travelers were very surprised when a band of apes seized them, and dragged them off to see their king. The King Ape had demanded that they be captured because he wanted to know what humans said about him and his subjects.

The travelers were taken into the king's

throne room. The king had commanded that all the apes be present to hear what humans said about them. The king sat on a throne — because that was what human kings did — and arranged his subjects in rows.

When the men were dragged in, the king asked, "What sort of a king do I seem to be to you, O strangers?"

The lying traveler replied, "You seem to me a most mighty king."

"And what is your opinion of those you see around me?" the King Ape asked.

"These," the lying traveler answered, "are worthy companions of yours, fit at least to be ambassadors and leaders of armies."

The ape and all his court were pleased with the lies. They commanded that a handsome present be given to the flatterer. On this, the truthful traveler thought to himself, 'If so great a reward be given for a lie, how may I be treated, if, according to my custom, I tell the truth?'

The King Ape turned to the truthful traveler. "And how do I and my friends seem to you?" he demanded.

"You are," the truthful traveler answered, "a most excellent ape. And all of your companions, who are copying you, are all excellent apes too."

The King Ape, enraged at this, threw the traveler to his furious fellow apes.

Don't always assume that the values of others match your own.

The Flea
and the
Man

There was once a tiny flea that bit a man again and again – it would not give up. The man suffered it for a long time, but finally he could take no more. He looked everywhere on himself until he found the flea and at last succeeded in catching it. Holding it between his finger and thumb, he said, "Who are you, wretched little creature, that you dare to cause me such misery?"

Now the flea was not so bold. It whimpered in a weak little voice, "Oh, sir! I beg of you, let me go, don't kill me! I am such a little thing that I can't do you much harm."

But the man said, "I am going to kill you at once. Whatever is bad has got to be destroyed. It doesn't matter how little harm it may cause."

Do not waste your pity on a scamp.

The Deer
in the
Ox-stall

There **was once a deer** who lived in a forest. His home was in some high crags amongst the trees, where he felt quite safe. But one day, to his horror, he heard hounds approaching. He was forced to flee, as the hounds chased him through the forest and out towards a nearby village.

The desperate deer galloped into a farmyard and dashed into a stable where a number of oxen were gathered. He looked around in terror for a hiding place, and in the end buried himself

under a pile of hay in an empty stall. He lay there, as still and silent as he could, hidden except for the very tips of his antlers.

After a few minutes, one of the oxen looked at the heap of hay and said, "Whatever made you come in here? The huntsmen who are after you may not find you, but you are running the risk of being captured by the village cattle herders."

Then the deer replied, "Please, let me stay for now. When night comes I shall easily escape under cover of darkness."

So the oxen went back to minding their own business and left the deer to his hiding.

That afternoon,

several farm-hands came to tend the oxen, but none noticed the deer. He began to relax, congratulating himself on his escape, and he thanked the oxen for letting him stay.

"We wish you well," said one oxen, "but you are not out of danger yet. If the master comes, you will certainly be found, for nothing ever escapes his keen eyes."

Sure enough, in came the master and made a great to-do about the way the oxen were kept. "The beasts are starving," he cried, "here, give them more hay." As he spoke, he seized an armful himself from the pile where the deer lay hidden, and at once found him. Calling his men, he caught and killed the deer, ready for eating.

There is no eye like the master's.

The Farmer, his Boy and the Crows

A **farmer once sowed** a field of wheat. He kept watch over it, for lots of rooks kept settling and eating the grain. With him went his boy, carrying a slingshot, so the farmer could scare the birds away. But whenever the farmer asked for the slingshot the birds understood what he said, and they were off in a moment.

"My boy," said the farmer, "we must get

the better of these birds. From now on, when I want the slingshot, I'll just say 'Humph!' and you must pass it to me quickly."

The flock soon came back. "Humph!" said the farmer. Of course, the birds took no notice, but the boy handed the farmer the slingshot, and he had time to fire several stones among them before they got away.

As the birds escaped they met some cranes, who asked them what the matter was. "It's those men!" said one crow. "They say one thing and mean another, which has just been the death of some of our friends."

Beware of people who say one thing but mean another.

The Lion, the Fox and the Deer

There was once a lion who was very ill. He lay in his den, barely able to move, starving for he could not hunt. One day, the fox paid him a visit. The desperate lion asked for some help.

"Please go to the nearby wood and trick the deer who lives there to come to my den. I am craving tasty deer for my dinner."

So the fox went to the

wood and found the deer, and said to him, "My dear sir, you're in luck. The lion, our king, is at the point of death, and has appointed you to be his successor to rule over the beasts. Now I must go back to him, and if you take my advice, you'll come too and be with him in his last moments."

The deer was flattered at being chosen to be the next king. He followed the fox to the lion's den. No sooner had he got inside than the lion sprang on him. But he was weak from lack of food and the deer got away with only his ears torn.

The lion begged the fox to have another try at coaxing the deer to his den.

"It'll be impossible this time," said the fox, "but I'll try." And off he went to the wood again.

The fox found the deer resting, recovering from his fright. When he saw the fox he cried, "What do you mean by trying to lure me to my

death? Go now, or I'll kill you with my antlers."

But the fox replied, "What a coward you are." "The lion meant no harm. He was only going to whisper some royal secrets into your ear when you went off like a scared rabbit. He might make the wolf king instead, unless you come back and show some spirit. I promise he won't hurt you."

The deer was foolish enough to return. This time the lion overpowered him, and enjoyed his dinner. When the lion wasn't looking, the fox stole the deer's brains as a reward for his trouble. When the lion began searching for them, the fox said, "I don't think there's much point in looking for the brains — a creature who twice walked into a lion's den couldn't have had any."

Be careful not to make the same mistake twice.